Jeannie & Genie

RELAX TO THE MAX

BY **TRISH GRANTED**

ILLUSTRATED BY **MANUELA LÓPEZ**

LITTLE SIMON

New York London Toronto Sydney New Delhi

 **LITTLE SIMON**

An imprint of Simon & Schuster Children's Publishing Division · 1230 Avenue of the Americas, New York, New York 10020 · First Little Simon hardcover edition January 2021

Copyright © 2021 by Simon & Schuster, Inc.

All rights reserved, including the right of reproduction in whole or in part in any form.

LITTLE SIMON is a registered trademark of Simon & Schuster, Inc., and associated colophon is a trademark of Simon & Schuster, Inc.

For information about special discounts for bulk purchases, please contact Simon & Schuster Special Sales at 1-866-506-1949 or business@simonandschuster.com.

The Simon & Schuster Speakers Bureau can bring authors to your live event. For more information or to book an event contact the Simon & Schuster Speakers Bureau at 1-866-248-3049 or visit our website at www.simonspeakers.com.

Designed by Brittany Fetcho

Manufactured in the United States of America 1120 FFG

10 9 8 7 6 5 4 3 2 1

Cataloging-in-Publication Data for this title is available from the Library of Congress.

ISBN 978-1-5344-7469-7 (hc)

ISBN 978-1-5344-7468-0 (pbk)

ISBN 978-1-5344-7470-3 (eBook)

TABLE OF CONTENTS

SPACE CADET

Jeanie Bell knew that look.

The twinkle in her best friend Willow Davis's eye could only mean one thing. Willow had something on her mind. Something that *wasn't* the science project they were supposed to be working on.

"Why did the cow dream of becoming an astronaut?" Willow asked as she put glow-in-the-dark star stickers on her cheeks.

"I don't know," Jeanie said with a sigh.

"Because it wanted to see the mooooooooon!" Willow joked.

Jeanie tried to smile. Willow had come over Sunday afternoon to help Jeanie make a 3-D map of the solar system. But she'd spent the last hour smooshing the clay they needed to make the planets into necklace charms and colorful bracelets.

"Um, maybe we should save some of that clay," said Jeanie.

Their second-grade teacher. Ms. Patel, expected them to present their science projects at the end of the week, and Jeanie was a little nervous about talking in front of the class. So she wanted to be sure their model was extra perfect since she would be the one presenting.

Willow wasn't as focused on grades or homework as Jeanie. But she was super creative and super silly. It was hard to believe that they were best friends.

Actually, a lot of things were hard to believe about Willow. Like the fact that she was actually . . . a genie. Yes, a magical genie. She was still in training, though. And she needed all the wish-granting practice she could get if she wanted to earn enough skill badges to become a Master Genie.

And Jeanie was the perfect person to help. She truly believed in the phrase "practice makes perfect." And wish-granting practice was pretty fun, too! One time, Jeanie

wished for a pizza, and Willow made it instantly appear!

Thinking about pizza made Jeanie's stomach growl. Luckily, it was time for dinner. The girls headed downstairs to the dining room.

"How's the space mission going?" Jeanie's mom asked.

"It's out of this world!" said Willow as she scratched Jeanie's dog, Bear.

"Well, we still have a lot of work to do." Jeanie sighed.

Jeanie's little brother, Jake, stared at Willow. "What are those rings around your wrist?"

"Let's call them the rings of Saturn!" said Willow, jangling her homemade bracelets.

"That's dopey," said Jake. He was six and always said everything he was thinking. "The only ring that matters is a race car track. *Vroom vroom!*" Jake jumped out of his chair and started racing around the table at top speed.

"Don't be rude," Jeanie scolded Jake.

"It's okay," said Willow.

She slipped the bracelets off and mushed them into a big ball of clay. "Now your racetrack is the only ring in town."

"Who's hungry?" called Jeanie's dad as he came in from the kitchen and placed a huge bowl of spaghetti on the table.

"Me! Me! Me!" cried Jake.

Just then Bear sniffed the clay ball and took a tiny bite.

Willow giggled. "I guess Bear is hungry too," she said.

But Jeanie didn't feel like laughing. That clay blob was supposed to be Neptune!

Chapter 2

NO TIME FOR FUN

On Monday morning Willow bounced into classroom 2B with a spring in her step.

The sun was shining. The birds were singing. And Willow was wearing her lucky outfit: a yellow sunburst dress, and sneakers with rainbow laces. She had a feeling today was going to be special.

But then, every day felt special to Willow.

"Everyone, take your seats," Ms. Patel told the class. "Today we're going to talk about geography. Who can tell me what our state capital is?"

Jeanie's hand shot into the air.

Willow grinned. Jeanie knew just about everything!

But after answering the next three questions, Ms. Patel asked Jeanie to take a break.

"How about you try this one, Max," said Ms. Patel. "If Lucy is traveling from Alaska to Florida, which direction is she going?"

Max tapped his chin. "I don't know . . . Al-ask-a friend Flori-da answer!"

Everyone cracked up—even Ms. Patel.

Well, everyone except Jeanie. Willow saw a dark scowl appear on her friend's face. She knew exactly what Jeanie was thinking. Max Mercado was always joking around. Didn't he know that learning was serious business?

"Actually," said Max, "Lucy is traveling southeast."

"That's correct," said Ms. Patel. "Well done, Max!"

Willow glanced at Jeanie. The scowl on her face was getting deeper by the second.

At recess, Willow found Jeanie sitting under her favorite tree—a big oak with low-hanging branches that created a secret spot. But instead of leaves, Jeanie was surrounded by papers!

"What are you doing?" asked Willow.

"Getting a head start on my homework," Jeanie said without looking up. "We're going to need every minute after school to finish our science project."

Just then a big red kickball came bouncing toward Jeanie.

Max ran over and caught the ball right before it crashed into Jeanie's homework.

"Couldyoubealittlemorecareful?" Jeanie huffed.

"Sorry," said Max. "Hey, do you guys want to play kickball with us?"

Willow liked that idea! "That sounds like fu—"

"No way!" Jeanie interrupted. "There's too much to do."

Max shrugged. "Okay. Maybe next time," he said with a smile. Then he ran back to the kickball field.

"You know . . . sometimes a break is nice," Willow told Jeanie. But she could tell Jeanie was already busy reading. She hadn't heard a word Willow had said.

She never has any time for fun, Willow thought. *Maybe it wouldn't be so bad if Jeanie could take a page out of Max's book.* Ha! A page out of Max's book! Willow laughed quietly at her own joke.

Chapter 3

THROWN FOR A LOOP

After school, the girls went to Jeanie's house to work on their project.

Jeanie wanted to get straight down to business. But as usual, Willow liked to ease into business.

"Max seems nice," said Willow. "What's he like?"

"Funny, popular, *and* smart," grumbled Jeanie. "His grades are just as good as mine. But he doesn't take *anything* seriously."

"He definitely knows how to have fun," agreed Willow.

Jeanie frowned. "He doesn't even try that hard. And yet, everything always works out perfectly for him." She sighed. Thinking about Max was just distracting her from her work. "Now let's get back to the project. This universe isn't going to build itself."

Jeanie scanned her room.

"Hey, where's the poster board?"
Jeanie asked. "We need to make the
galaxy background."

Willow snapped her finger and
said, "I think I saw some in the den
with Jake."

Jeanie rolled her eyes. Her little brother was always taking her stuff. She had a bad feeling about this.

She rushed downstairs and followed the *vroom, vroom, vroom* sounds into the den. Or what *used* to be the den. Jake had turned the room into a racetrack! A huge loop ran in front of the couch, under the coffee table, and past the window— and it was all made out of Jeanie's poster board and clay.

"You ruined the whole solar system!" Jeanie shouted at her brother.

29

"I did not, Meanie Jeanie!" Jake insisted. "I made it better!"

"How will we ever finish our project?" cried Jeanie.

Just then, Willow rushed into the den.

"Don't worry!" Willow told Jeanie. "We can fix this. Everything's going to be fine."

Jeanie knew her friend was trying to help . . . but it wasn't working. She felt her lower lip begin to tremble.

"Try to take a breath," Willow suggested. "Maybe you could think about what Max would do in this situation. I bet he would tell himself to just relax."

Those words unlocked something inside Jeanie. The project was going to be a disaster, her partner wanted to make jewelry all day, her little brother had ruined her poster

board . . . and *she* was supposed to *just relax*?

"Just relax? Just relax!" she cried, looking directly into Willow's eyes. "I wish I could relax as easily as Max . . . but that's not me!"

Suddenly a flash of golden light lit up the room.

Jeanie took a step back . . . right into her mom.

Mrs. Bell looked around the den. Jake sat on the couch staring at his race cars guiltily, Willow looked shocked, and Jeanie was about to cry.

"Okay, I think everyone needs a
break," Mrs. Bell said kindly. "Jake,
please set the table for dinner. Girls,
I want you to take the rest of the
night off."

Jeanie's mom helped Willow into
her coat, and the two girls walked
to the front door.

"See you tomorrow?" Willow
asked.

Jeanie nodded and gave her a half-hearted wave.

She'd spent the whole day pouring her energy into schoolwork.

But suddenly she didn't feel like doing *anything* anymore.

A NEW JEANIE IN TOWN

The next morning Willow worried all the way to school.

She hated that she had made Jeanie so upset yesterday.

Plus there had been that golden flash. When a wish was granted, Willow's magic lamp necklace would light up. So a wish must have been granted yesterday. The problem was . . . since Willow was still in training, her wishes didn't always go the way they should.

Willow heard loud laughter coming from classroom 2B. It sounded more like a comedy club than an elementary school!

She opened the door and saw the whole class crowded around Jeanie. She was telling a story, and everyone was listening eagerly—even the class hamster, Jelly Bean!

"So my little brother Jake made a racetrack out of my poster of the galaxy," Jeanie said. "I'll bet he even used my clay to make a parking *meteor*!"

Everyone laughed hysterically. Some classmates were practically in tears from laughing!

Willow was shocked. Here was Jeanie, *laughing* about their unfinished science project! This didn't seem like her at all.

And another thing: Jeanie didn't *look* like herself either. Her hair stuck up in all directions. She had on two different shoes—one ballet flat and one sneaker. And she wore a paint-splattered sweatshirt … over pajamas!

Ms. Patel cleared her throat. "Okay, class! Today we're going to talk about the solar system. Who's ready to blast into space?"

"Not me!" shouted Jeanie. "I left my asteroid belt at home!"

The whole class laughed, including Ms. Patel.

But as soon as they started the lesson, Willow saw the energy drain out of Jeanie. First she yawned. Then she slumped. And she didn't raise her hand once.

All morning, Willow watched Jeanie act very un-Jeanie-like. During math, she kicked off her shoes and sat cross-legged in her chair. She doodled all through social studies. And when she passed a note during reading time, Willow knew something was wrong.

"What's going on with you?" Willow asked as the class lined up for lunch.

Jeanie shrugged and said, "I took your advice. Remember? You told me to relax like Max. So watch out, universe. There's a new Jeanie in town. Now, who has two thumbs and is totally hungry for cafeteria fish sticks?"

Jeanie pointed her thumbs at herself and shouted, "This girl!"

Willow's jaw dropped. No one liked the cafeteria fish sticks. Not since they'd taken down the whole fourth grade.

Sure, Willow had wanted Jeanie to loosen up . . . but this spell had gone too far.

Willow *had* to figure out a way to get Jeanie out of her wish!

Chapter 5

TACO TUESDAY

By the end of the day, Jeanie was still feeling totally relaxed.

She took a catnap on the bus home. Then, verrrry slowly, she opened her front door.

"Mom! I'm hoooooooome!" Jeanie yelled.

"I'm in the den!" Mrs. Bell replied.

It took Jeanie a full five minutes to walk down the hall.

"How was school today, sweetie?" her mom asked.

Jeanie started to tell her mom what she'd learned. Then she stopped. For some reason she didn't feel like talking about school. "Hey, when are we going on a family vacation?"

Her mom looked puzzled. "We don't have any family trips coming up."

"Why?" said Jeanie. "I *need* a vacation!"

Jeanie could picture herself lying on a sandy beach. Or floating in a pool. Or taking a nap in a hammock between two shady trees.

"For now, let's focus on dinner," said Jeanie's mom as she walked to the kitchen. "I'm going to start making my homemade salsa. It's Taco Tuesday!"

Jeanie yawned and looked out the window. Bear was rolling around in a sunny patch of grass.

That looks awesome! Jeanie thought. So awesome that she decided to go out back and roll around in the sun too.

Jeanie wiggled her toes in the grass, showed Bear the clouds that looked like bunnies, and hummed along to the sounds of trumpet practice coming from Mr. Penny's house next door.

Jake watched his sister, then finally poked his head outside to ask, "Hey, what are you doing?"

"What does it look like I'm doing?" she answered. "I'm *taking it easy*."

"Mom!" Jake yelled. "I think Jeanie's broken."

"Am not," said Jeanie. She stuck her tongue out.

"Meanie Jeanie strikes again," said Jake.

"I heard that," their mom's voice called through the window. "Jeanie, come set the table for dinner, please."

"In a min-uuuuuuute!" Jeanie could hardly believe those words were coming out of her mouth. But the sunshine was so warm, and the grass felt so nice.

This time her mom's voice was kind but firm. "Now, please!"

Jeanie entered the dining room as slow as a turtle. There was a stack of plates and silverware on the table. She picked up a fork. Eating at the table was so formal! There *had* to be a way to make dinner a little more laid back.

That's it! Jeanie thought. *We'll lie back!*

She carried the plates and silverware into the den. Then she threw all the couch cushions on the floor. Lying back on the carpet during dinner was going to be super relaxing.

Jeanie's Den Diner was open for business . . .

. . . until Jake crashed one of his cars into the diner.

"Hey! This isn't setting the table," he said. "You're gonna be in so much trouble!"

"Who cares?" Jeanie laughed, cool as a cucumber. "This'll be more fun!"

Luckily, Jeanie's parents thought so too. Tonight the Bells were doing Taco Tuesday picnic style!

Chapter 6

SLOW MOTION

The next morning Willow looked for Jeanie by the cubbies.

She yawned like she'd never yawned before. Willow had barely slept. She'd spent the whole night looking through her mom's library for a way to get Jeanie back to normal.

Willow's mom was the director of the World Genie Association (WGA) and had all the magic books a genie could wish for. Willow had found lots of information about relaxation wishes, but nothing about how to undo them.

She'd even tried gazing into the Davis family's crystal ball. If she could see the future, she'd know what to do. But Willow hadn't earned her future-telling badge yet, so all she saw in the crystal ball was her own reflection.

Maybe she should just give up and let the magic run its course?

But when Willow spotted Jeanie looking just as sloppy as she had the day before, she knew giving up was not an option.

"How are you?" she asked Jeanie.

"Fine . . . I think," said Jeanie. "My head's just sort of . . . cloudy. And my legs feel like wet noodles. Do you ever wonder what would happen if we forgot how to walk? We'd have to just crawl around and—"

"Do you think our geography quiz will have questions about the state capitals?" Willow asked quickly.

Normally when Willow brought up a test, Jeanie would give unending advice about the chapters they needed to read, her favorite study strategies, and a reminder to bring a sharpened pencil.

But this Jeanie was *not* acting normally.

"Oh, I don't knooooow," she said as she dragged out the word "know."

Willow's eyes went wide. Jeanie was stuck in slow motion!

"I sound sooooo weird," Jeanie exclaimed. "It's like I'm a slooooth." Jeanie smiled lazily, then turned to stare out the window.

Ms. Patel clapped her hands twice to get everyone's attention. "Class, let's open our science textbooks to chapter three."

Jeanie slowly raised her hand. "Ms. Patel, could we work outside today?" she asked. "It's soooooo nice out."

Now Willow was super worried.

Working outside would be Normal Jeanie's nightmare, with all the distractions. But this wasn't Normal Jeanie.

Ms. Patel didn't seem to notice. "That's a lovely idea, Jeanie!"

As class headed outside, Max caught up with Jeanie and Willow.

"This is awesome," he told Jeanie. "All these books were getting too stuffy for me."

"Right?" said Jeanie. "Who needs books anyway?"

Willow gulped. Jeanie *loved* books. Like, more than anything in the world. Ugh. Ever since Jeanie made the wish, everything about her was wrong, wrong, wrong!

How would Willow ever make things right?

Chapter 7

CHANGING COLORS

Outside, Jeanie twirled a leaf in her hands.

"The yellow ones are amazing," said Max. "That tree looks like it's glowing!"

"I like the red leaves best," said Jeanie. "Willow likes orange."

Willow smiled, then asked, "Hey, Jeanie. How do leaves know when to change color?"

"That's easy. Leaves have a green pigment in them that uses light to make food. When the days get shorter, they stop getting enough light, and their green color disappears," Jeanie said.

Then she blinked. Where had *that* come from?

"I was going to tell a fall joke," said Willow, "but hearing you tell fall facts is even better!" She hugged Jeanie.

Jeanie yawned. She was suddenly extremely tired. But before she could doze off, Ms. Patel asked the class, "Can anyone tell us why trees change color in the fall?"

No one raised their hand.

Jeanie felt someone tapping her shoulder. She turned. Willow was motioning for her to talk. But Jeanie had no idea why.

Finally, Willow spoke up. "Um, Jeanie was just talking about that."

"Would you like to share the answer with us?" Ms. Patel asked Jeanie.

A fog settled in Jeanie's brain. She was sure she knew the answer. But when she opened her mouth, all that came out was a yawn!

Max looked at Jeanie with a confused expression on his face. Then he raised his hand.

"Because they don't get enough light," he said. "The green part of a leaf needs light to make food. When they don't get it, they turn yellow or orange or red or brown."

Jeanie knew that! But why couldn't she say it? Something weird was going on. . . .

When the class broke into groups to collect leaf samples, Jeanie pulled Willow aside.

"What is wrong with me?" she demanded.

Willow looked worried. But before she could say anything, Jeanie heard a birdsong from the tree. She spotted a robin hopping in the leaves. The next thing she knew, Jeanie was hopping along too, flapping and clapping and chirping a silly song.

Jeanie's bird dance made everyone crack up.

Everyone except Ms. Patel. "Jeanie, you'll have to wait for recess to get that energy out," she scolded. "Now please focus."

Jeanie's cheeks felt hot. She wasn't used to getting in trouble!

Willow took her by the shoulders and whispered in her ear. "Don't be mad, but you made a wish . . . to be more relaxed . . . and it came true."

"No, no, no," Jeanie whispered back. "We've got to do something to fix this."

"You could try making another wish," suggested Willow.

"That's a good idea," said Jeanie. She looked directly into Willow's eyes and said, "I wish everything was back to normal!"

But nothing happened. No flash. No magic. Nothing.

"Oh no," gasped Willow. "A wish only works if the person really wants it to come true. Maybe deep down you really like the new you."

Jeanie shook her head. She definitely did *not* like the new her.

"Leave it to me," said Willow. "I may be new to wish granting, but I've still got a few more tricks up my sleeve."

Chapter 8

REVERSE THE CURSE

The next day before PE, Willow told Jeanie her first idea: the anti-relax plan!

"What is the *least* relaxing thing you can think of?" she whispered as they walked toward the gym. "Maybe if we do that, the spell will cancel itself out."

Jeanie was silent for a moment. Then she grimaced.

"Dodgeball," she replied. "I hate dodgeball."

Willow nodded. She was pretty sure that would do the trick!

Once they got to gym class, Willow raised her hand right away. "Ms. Martinez, can we play dodgeball?" she asked.

The Lee triplets cheered.

"Actually, we haven't played that in a while," Ms. Martinez said. She blew her whistle. "Dodgeball it is!"

But when they started playing, Willow realized her plan was doomed.

Instead of freezing up, the relaxed Jeanie danced and leaped across the gym like an acrobat, dodging every ball.

And worse, Jeanie was doing it with a smile. Even her least favorite sport couldn't ruin her relaxed vibe.

Willow would have to think of something else—fast.

Since fighting the spell hadn't worked, Willow decided that after school they should try idea number two: Relax to the max!

★*★

"Let's do all the calming things we can think of, all at one time. It might get the spell out of your system!" she told Jeanie. "What are the best ways to relax?"

"When my dad wants to relax, he naps in a hammock," Jeanie replied. "Mom cooks. And Jake reads comic books."

"Coloring makes me feel peaceful," added Willow. "And my mom spins a distant star on its side.

But I'm not sure we should try that without adult genie supervision."

"I like yoga," Jeanie said. "Silently practicing for the spelling bee between oms clears my head."

"Let's do it!" said Willow.

They searched through the house, gathering a pot and wooden spoon, comics, and a coloring book and crayons, along with a couple of cucumber slices from the fridge. Then they headed outside.

Jeanie lay in the hammock. Soon she was stirring a pot of crayons, trying to read a comic book from underneath two cucumber slices, and chanting, "Om!"

"Are you relaxed yet?" Willow whispered.

Jeanie was about to answer when Jake stormed through the back door with Bear.

"Hey! That's my comic book!" he yelled. "Give it back!"

Jake grabbed the comic just as Bear jumped into the hammock and licked the cucumber slices that were over Jeanie's eyes.

"Wow, I'm actually totally cool with all this happening to me," said Jeanie breezily.

Willow slumped down, defeated. If Jeanie was still relaxed after that, it meant the relax-to-the-max plan was a bust.

What else could Willow do? She dragged Jeanie upstairs, found the clay and poster board, and got to work. Willow couldn't break the spell, but at least she could finish their solar system project.

When Willow was done, she asked, "Do you think we should practice your presentation for tomorrow?"

"Relax," said Jeanie, smiling serenely. "Things will work out. They always do."

Willow hoped her friend was right.

Chapter 9

ECLIPSED

When Jeanie's alarm clock went off Friday morning, she hit the snooze button.

She hit it again a few minutes later. And a few minutes after that. It felt good to take it easy. After all, what was the rush?

Finally, she stretched lazily and got out of bed, slipping a comfy hoodie on over her pajamas.

Downstairs, she ate a few bites of pancake and played slingshot with her blueberries.

Then she slung her empty backpack over her shoulder. Jeanie felt like she was forgetting something, but she couldn't think what.

"Oh well," she said to herself as she headed for the door.

"Hey!" yelled Jake. "Isn't your science presentation today?"

He held up her model of the solar system. She'd almost left it behind!

"What? Oh yeah," said Jeanie. "Thanks, Jake. That's so sweet of you to remind me." She ruffled her brother's hair.

Jake's jaw dropped. Jeanie was never that nice to him, especially first thing in the morning.

Jeanie's good mood continued all the way to school. She was peaceful during morning announcements, serene during roll call, and totally trouble free as Ms. Patel asked the class to get their presentations ready.

She didn't even flinch when Max's group gave a practically perfect demonstration of a solar eclipse.

Then it was her turn. Normally, Jeanie was nervous about speaking in front of the class, but this time was different. She calmly explained the solar system . . . along with a few surprise jokes.

THE SOLAR SYSTEM

"Why did Mickey Mouse name his dog Pluto?" she asked the class. "Because he's not a planet!"

Once everyone stopped laughing, Jeanie continued.

"That's right—Pluto used to be the ninth planet," she explained, showing off the necklace Willow had made. "But it got bumped. That's why we made it an accessory!"

Jeanie could see Willow smiling.

At the end of science class, Ms. Patel came around to give each group feedback.

"Well done," Ms. Patel told the girls. "That was very creative. And, Jeanie, your presentation skills have come a long way. You both get an A!"

Jeanie gave Willow a high five. They'd done it!

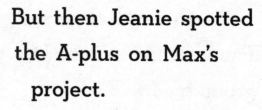

But then Jeanie spotted the A-plus on Max's project.

All of a sudden she felt . . . well . . . eclipsed. Could it be that she wasn't the best student in classroom 2B?

No! That wasn't right. A bolt of energy burst inside Jeanie like her own personal big bang. Millions of questions sprang to her mind, and she wanted to know the answers to all of them.

Jeanie leaned over to Willow and whispered, "Hey, I wonder how big the universe is. And why the sky is blue. And how constellations get their names. Or what the difference between an asteroid and a comet and a meteor is. Or what star is closest to the sun. But mostly I wonder how in the world Max got an A-plus, and we got a lousy A!"

Willow smiled as a golden beam flashed and Jeanie returned back to normal.

OUT OF THIS WORLD

At recess later that day, Willow found Jeanie under her favorite oak tree.

"Jeanie, are you okay?" she asked cautiously.

Jeanie shrugged. "I'm wearing pajamas . . . at school! My hair's a mess, my backpack is empty, and I definitely haven't done my math homework," she said. "So not exactly

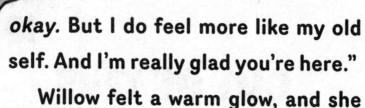

okay. But I do feel more like my old self. And I'm really glad you're here."

Willow felt a warm glow, and she launched herself at Jeanie, giving her best friend a giant hug.

"Okay, okay," said Jeanie. "Best-friend hugs have a thirty-second time limit."

Willow stepped back. "You really *are* back to normal, huh?" she joked.

Jeanie winked. "Just kidding," she said, pulling Willow back into a hug.

Then Jeanie said seriously, "Thank you for finishing our project. The poster looked so great!"

"Thanks," said Willow. "But the presentation part was all you. You were fantastic!"

"Well, I guess it wasn't so bad that I was a little more relaxed than usual," Jeanie said with a smile. "But we've still got a lot of work to do on your wish-granting!"

Willow nodded. "I'm just glad you didn't wish you could *chill out*," she joked. "I might have sent you to the North Pole!"

The two girls burst into giggles. But then Jeanie stopped. "Wait. You're kidding right? Please tell me you're just kidding, Willow."

"Totally kidding," Willow said. Then she thought for a minute. "I mean, I'd never do that *on purpose*. But I could definitely use a little more practice. If I promise to work on spell control, will you promise to work on balancing schoolwork with relaxing?"

"Deal!" said Jeanie.

Willow smiled. "Hey, want to go spend the rest of recess in the library?"

Jeanie nodded and stood up. "I *am* suddenly curious about how to build an igloo and avoid frostbite," she said. "You know . . . just in case."

Willow laughed. "You are as practical as ever," she said.

Willow was the happiest she'd been all week. Having her friend back felt out of this world!

LOOK FOR MORE

Jeanie & Genie

BOOKS AT YOUR FAVORITE STORE!